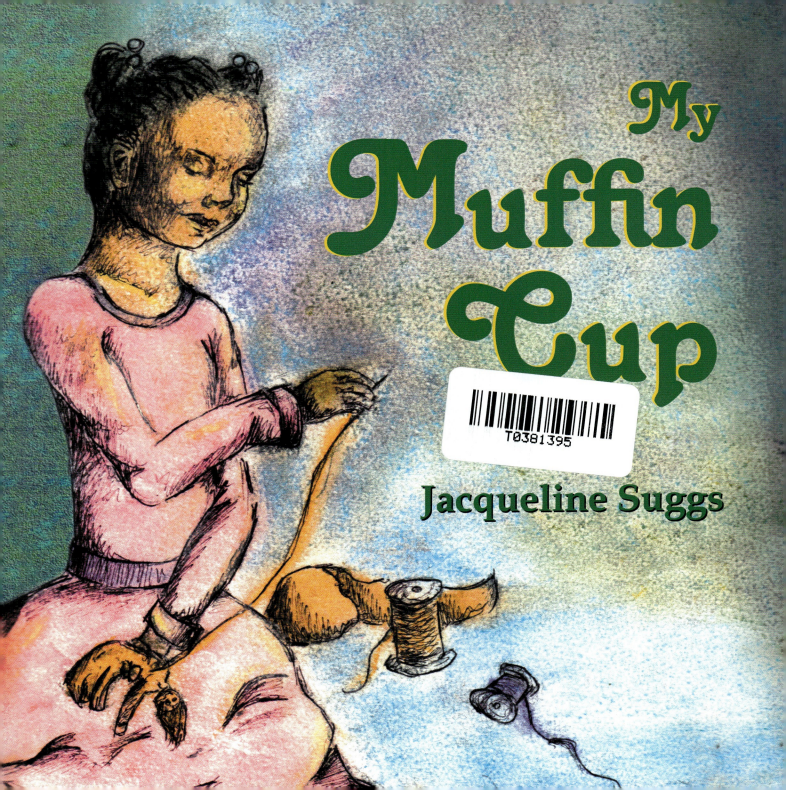

My Muffin Cup

Jacqueline Suggs

To order additional copies of this book, contact:
Xlibris
1-888-795-4274
www.Xlibris.com
Orders@Xlibris.com

Muffin Cup received her nickname from her grandma, Her birth name is Collie Mae Bell. Muffin Cup is a very wise little girl just like her grandma. Often, people would walk by Muffin Cup asking, "How are you feeling today?" Muffin Cup always replied, "I'm blessed more and more each day", as she continued her routine.

3

Muffin Cup is always helping out at home where her grandma works as a housekeeper. In the small town of Shady Oak, everyone called grandma "Granny". Granny works for Mr. and Mrs. Little. The Little's make their living by growing corn on their 15 acres of land. Mr. and Mrs. Little have one son named Jeff Rufus. The people around Shady Oak think he's the greatest kid in town. Jeff Rufus had a thing for sneaking in the cornfield eating ears of corn, he loved it!

His father thought the bugs were eating his corn, although his crop was always treated for bugs and he'd never seen a bug in the cornfield. One day Mr. Little saw his son eating his corn in the field and realized that the bug was his son. From that day little Jeff Rufus was called by his nickname "Corn".

Granny:	*walks to the kitchen saying to everyone* Good morning.
Mr. & Mrs. Little:	Good morning Granny
Granny:	Today is Saturday. What would you two like for dinner?
Mrs. Little:	say fried corn, corn muffins, baked chicken, potato salad, and for dessert strawberry ice cream?
Granny:	Yes mam! A very good choice for today!

Granny called Muffin Cup to the kitchen

Granny:	Muffin Cup would you like to ride with me to the grocery store?
Muffin Cup:	Yes Granny, but what for? Today is Saturday, we never go to the store on Saturday.
Granny:	Well child, we need ice cream for dessert.
Muffin Cup:	Well, if we don't have ice cream at the house, going to the store is a wise thing to do, right Granny?

7

Granny: Yes child!

Granny driving to the store with Muffin Cup

Muffin Cup: Granny, are you thinking
                    of other things to buy
                    while we are at the store?

Granny: No, because the only
                    thing we're missing at
                    home is ice cream.

Muffin Cup: We need to keep ice
                    cream at all times in all
                    flavors, Granny.

*After getting what they needed at the store
they arrive home. Granny sees Corn and
Mr. Little in the cornfield.*

Muffin Cup: Hi, Corn! Hi, Mr. Little!
                    (*as she waved at them*)

Mr. Little and corn both waved

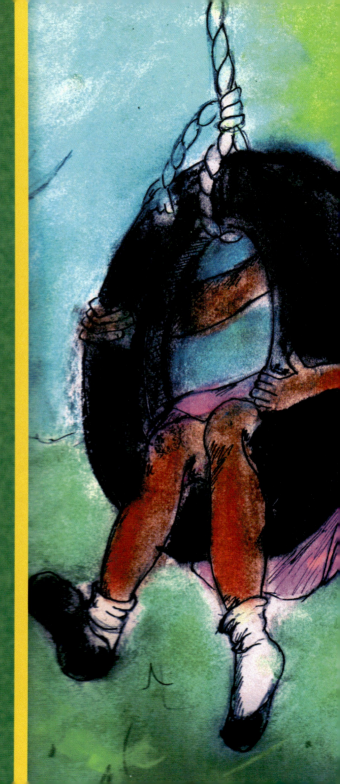

Muffin Cup: Granny! If Corn is eating the corn on cobs in the field, why is Mr. Little letting him go into the field with him?

Granny: So he can keep an eye on him and keep him busy.

Muffin Cup: Corn is going to be a healthy young man when he grows up.

Granny: Yes indeed! With the food this child puts in his belly, he is going to be healthy!

Entering into the house placing the ice cream in the freezer, Granny starts to cook dinner.

Muffin Cup: Granny, I want to go outside to play with the dog.

9

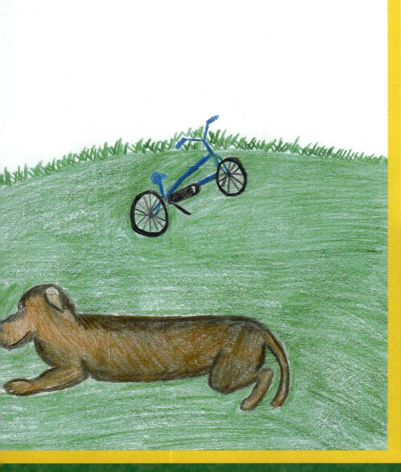
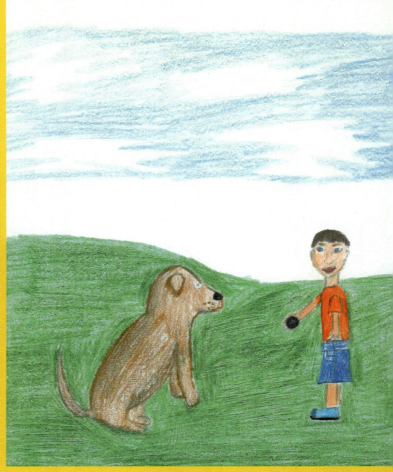

Granny: Yes you may go and
               be careful.

Muffin Cup: Yes Mam.

As she runs and plays with her dog time goes by. Dinner is ready and everyone is at the table eating.

Mr. Little: For some reason, Corn is not the only one
               eating up the cornfield

Mrs. Little: Why you say that dear?

Mr. Little: Well, someone is peeling the cob and leaving
               trails as they walk away and it's too many
               missing ears of corn for one boy to eat.

Mrs. Little:	Well, do you have an idea or could it be bugs.
Muffin Cup:	It could be a huge bug with two legs and two arms, with a new tactic of doing things.
Corn:	Muffin Cup you have so much to say and no one is listening.
Muffin Cup:	Why are you responding to me Corn? Could you have done such a thing Corn? Hmm-mmm.
Corn:	Sometimes Muffin Cup, you think too hard around here.
Granny:	Now, now children you two cacklin' like hens, eat your dinner.
Muffin Cup & Corn: Yes mam.	
Mr. Little:	When everyone is finished, we can all sit on the front porch for a little fresh air.

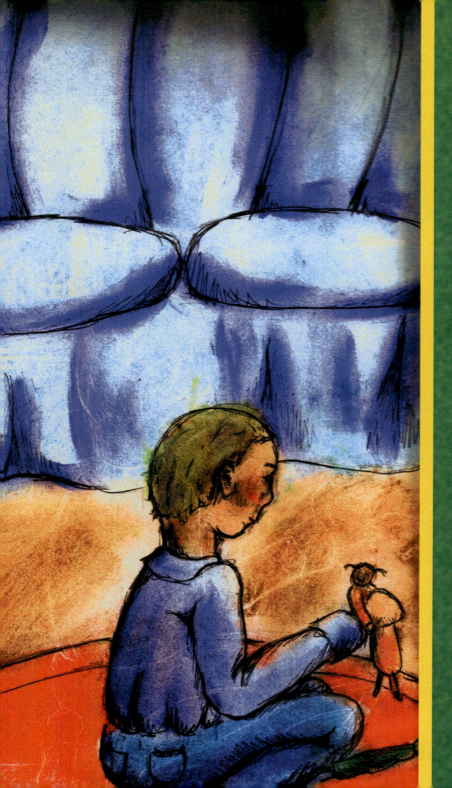

Corn:	Pa, Can I get a new bike to ride sometimes?
Mr. Little:	You will have to save every penny to buy anything you want.
Muffin Cup:	Corn, I have 50 cents to help you, that's if you want it. Now that is a start.

Corn:	Thank you so much.
Muffin Cup:	Now this is a blessing to you Corn. Someone is willing to help you. It's very hard to find a helping hand.
Corn:	I know.
Granny:	That's right little one so always help each other. But do not let anyone take advantage of you.

As the days go by, Corn figures out a way to earn money to buy his bike. If he sales five ears of corn to the neighbors for $3.50 each he will have plenty of money for the bike. Corn needs a total of $25 to buy his bike. His father has no idea what Corn is up to. Two weeks later Corn has made a huge profit, enough to buy a $50 bike. After spending the $50 on a bigger and better bike he will still have $30 left over. Corn went to his father and said.

Corn:	Pa, I'm ready to go and get my new bike.

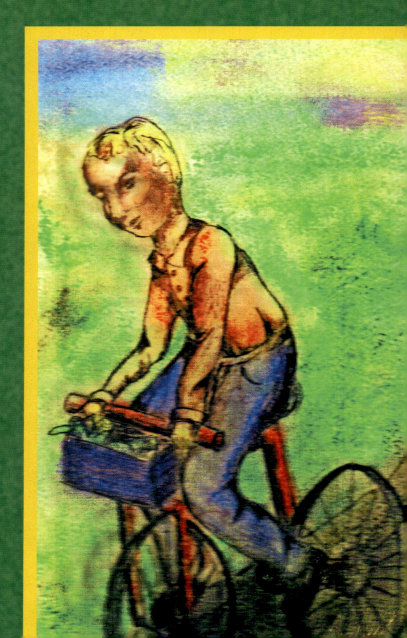

14

Mr. Little:	Well, how much you saved.
Corn:	$80.00
Mr. Little:	Son, how did you save so much?
Corn:	It was real hard.
Mr. Little:	We can go this weekend.
Corn:	Okay, thanks Pa.

Mr. Little Laughs, not knowing how Corn got the money, as Corn runs off with joy. Mr. Little thought hard but still couldn't figure it out.

As the day went by it was time for Corn to go with his dad to purchase his new bike.

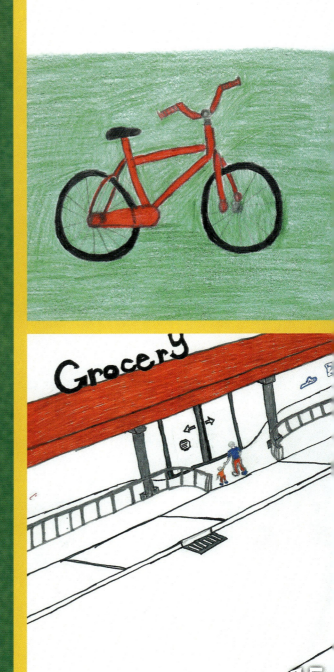

15

Corn: *(Smiling Happily)* Dad you are the best dad in the World, Thank You!

Mr. Little: And Corn you are the best son in the world.

Mr. Little: Son at your age, being only 8 years old, you are able to save money to get what you want. That's a wonderful thing! We all have to do things honestly in order to make it in the World. Everyone that wants to gain something in the future must also be a responsible person

Corn: What does that mean father.

Mr. Little: Well, however you earn enough money to buy this bike, if you had done something wrong to make this money, you would have to be responsible for the price to pay. "Like a punishment" do you understand now.

Corn: Yes father. Well all I did was sell ears of corn to neighborhood families. 5 ears for $3.50 a house.

Mr. Little Laughs

Mr. Little: How did you figure this out?

Corn: I just got to thinking and Pa it was the Lord who led me to do this. I figure if instead of me eating the corn I can sell it.

Mr. Little and Corn made it home with the new bike. Little Muffin Cup runs up to see Corn's new bike.

Muffin Cup: Hello Corn, I see your bike is very nice! When can I ride?

Corn: You can ride after me, just give me a little time.

Muffin Cup: Of course, Corn how much you saved up to get this bike?

Corn: $80.00 dollars, but the bike only costs me $50.00 dollars. I did not worry at all about getting the money. Just had to do things the right way. And I made it.

Muffin Cup: Child, you have done something so joyous. The Lord gave this to you and always remember what the Lord will do for you. All your desires will be answered. Just do not get greedy.

Corn: Muffin Cup you talk with good wisdom. Keep up the good work.

Muffin Cup: $80, you did wonderful! How did you get up the money?

Corn: I sold ears of corn.

Muffin Cup: Well, you ate enough corn to figure out something. And I say again that was a good way of thinking. You did very good.

Corn: Thank you so very much.

As Corn rides his bike in the backyard, Mrs. Little looks out the window and smiles.

Mrs. Little: That child will be a millionaire in the Lord's Word.

Granny: What makes you say that?

Mrs. Little: How he speaks about the Lord guiding him in earning money for that bike.

Granny: Yes, you might be very right about that.

Muffin Cup: Granny, can I get a bike or a doll?

Granny: Yes, you may if you save your money you can get anything you want when you go to the store. Look to see how much things cost and start saving for it.

Muffin Cup: Granny, I made a doll but if I can make more and sale them, can I purchase anything I want?

Granny: Now, you will have to share and budget every penny and have good measurement on fabric and anything else you will need.

Muffin Cup: Well, I know this will take a long time and perhaps this will pay off big for me. I know what I will have to do and now this is my official project.

While Granny and Muffin Cup are talking, Corn walks up, hearing the conversation as he replies:

Corn: I can help pull this along.

Muffin Cup: Yes, you can.

Corn: Lets go and raise money.

Muffin Cup: How?

Corn: Hush up and come on.

Muffin Cup follows Corn onto the front porch. Corn tells her his idea.

Muffin Cup: Did you get in trouble for selling your father's corn?

Corn: No!

Corn and Muffin Cup started selling corn from the field.
They sold to the entire community, everyone was buying corn!
These two characters were making a good name for themselves
The two were not aware of what was happening, they were now "popular". Mr. Little was astounded by his son's dedication to making money for the family. His father had no idea he was helping Muffin Cup.

Mr. Little: Corn is doing a wonderful job selling the corn.

Mrs. Little: Now this is a good thing for him at his age.

Mr. Little: Yeap. Yes in deed. This family has a big market in corn
                 now. Thanks to Corn.

*Mr. Little didn't know that Corn was selling his corn to help Muffin Cup buy
materials she needed for her doll making. The two of them collected plenty of
money to make the dolls. Once the dolls were made Muffin Cup sold them to
customers in the community. The dolls were very popular! One particular doll
named Tanny started a riot. Muffin Cup only made three Tanny dolls which
made this style rare.*

In the meantime, Mr. Little was still looking for the funds from the corn.

Mr. Little: Corn, How much did the family raise from the corn?

Corn: Father what are you talking about?

Mr. Little: You know, the money from the corn sale?

Corn: Father that money went towards the materials for Muffin
                 Cup's dolls she's selling to the community. She wants
                 to make a profit to buy things she wants and needs. She
                 doesn't have a ma' or pa' like me so we work together on
                 my bike and on her dolls. You understand don't you Pa'?

Mr. Little: Well now, I have a project that I'd like for you and Muffin
                 Cup to help me with.

Corn:	Well. Yes Father, what is it?
Mr. Little:	I want to save money for the winter, if any hard times come ahead we will have the money.
Corn:	Father that's a good idea. I will tell Muffin Cup.

Corn tells Muffin Cup about the idea. They agreed and started on Mr. Little's project. Corn and Muffin Cup wasn't aware of the huge fields they had to pick so the whole family joined in to help. This made Mr. Little very happy!

Corn:	Father I will start selling once we gather a lot of corn.
Mr. Little:	Corn, how are you coming up with a good price like that and selling every bag?
Corn:	Father, I just try to be fair with my customers as I'd want them to be with me.
Muffin Cup:	Corn, you are so true to yourself. We work hard together and it will pay off that's what I was taught by my Granny.
Granny:	Corn you are on my mind every day about selling so much corn.

22

Granny: Corn you did a good job! You deserve a pat on the back.

Muffin Cup: Now, now. Granny I deserve some praise. Do you not think so Corn.

Corn: (proudly says) Oh, yes. This is true Granny because you let her stand out with her wisdom and she passed it on to me.

Muffin Cup: But I do not need a praise or a pat on my back for good work that has been made by me.

Granny: Child you are so true to yourself.

Mr. Little: Corn and Muffin Cup you both deserve a reward for coming up with good ideas at such a young age.

Mrs. Little: Sweetheart they also learned how to share with one another which is very important in becoming a huge success.

Muffin Cup: My dolls will be called "Wisdom Dolls". They will have tan color and be the All American Wisdom Doll. I'll start making them as soon as we finish with Mr. Little's corn collecting so he can make his profit for the family. Next season he will start over and have a better crop of corn.

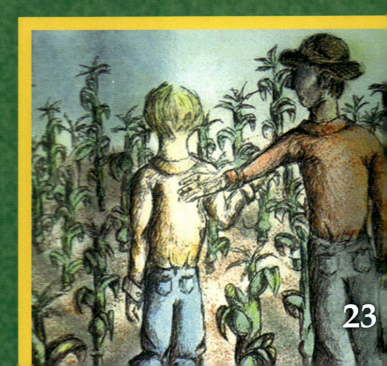

Mrs. Little:	When will you start little one?	Mr. Little:	Well go ahead and get started now if you know they will sell.
Muffin Cup:	Next month, but I have already made five. I sold two of them and my customers love the way they look. They will surely spread the word and come back for more.	Granny:	This child is full of potential has a good mind to do well. I'm so proud of her. My granddaughter!

Corn: Granny are you proud of me too?

Granny: Yes, I am, you are a wonderful child also.

As time goes by, the Littles are gathering and bagging corn for sale. Muffin Cup runs into her room to start making more dolls. Muffin Cup has dolls of different styles; some had dark hair like wool, curly hair, and straight hair. All of her dolls have tan colored skin because she wants them to represent different cultures. The clothing style she chose for her dolls is from the 18th Century, male and female attire.

Granny: Muffin Cup I'm coming up to see how you are coming along.

Muffin Cup: Everything is going just fine! I have to make the dresses, pants, and shirts for my dolls after I put the bodies together.

Granny: Do you need help, child?

Muffin Cup: No mam, but thank you though.

Granny: How are you going to advertise?

Muffin Cup: Take them to the store and set up there.

Granny: Now ask Mr. Whitfield if he could give a definite ok to set up.

Muffin Cup: I know he will, Granny, but as you say always ask first.

As months went by, Muffin Cup was ready to start selling her dolls. She got permission from Mr. Whitfield, giving her the o.k. to come and display the dolls.

Muffin Cup: Granny will you drive me to the store so I can set up?

Granny: Yes.

Mrs. Little: I will help you! How much you will sell them for?

Muffin Cup: $20.00 per doll.

Muffin Cup: Is this too much?

Mrs. Little: Why, no child! You have a masterpiece. Let's get started we have to be there time the store opens.

Gathering up the dolls putting them in boxes, Muffin Cup carefully wrapped them in plastic one by one.

Granny: Why did you put skin colors tan?

Muffin Cup: To satisfy all races because I do not have enough money for different colors of paint.

Muffin Cup: When I make enough money I'll be able to buy whatever color that is needed.

Granny: You are so true to yourself, go on thinking child!

Mrs. Little: Well, we are loaded and ready to go now.

Corn stands on the porch and wishes Muffin Cup good luck as he sees them off.

Mr. Whitfield is waiting for Muffin Cup to come. He waited very anxiously to see what her dolls look like. 15min. later they pull up. Mr. Whitfield runs to the car and helps them with the boxes.

Mr. Whitfield: May I take a look?

Mrs. Little: Yes.

Muffin Cup: Whatcha think, Mr. Whitfield?

Mr. Whitfield looks and took a deep breath biting his nails, happily and breathless.

Mr. Whitfield: This is a beautiful collection.

Mr. Whitfield puts all his energy on making a place for the dolls. He runs back and forth finding the perfect place for customers to see the dolls when they come in the store.

Mr. Whitfield: My little Muffin Cup, you have done a marvelous job!
Did anyone help you with these dolls? No one I know
could have done this all by themselves! How did you
do all of this?

Granny: She done this all by herself. I checked on her and she was
working on her own.

Mr. Whitfield: Well, you will sell everyone of them, I'll make sure of it!
You will not have to pay me anything. It's good to see a
little girl with so much talent. I'm hoping you will make
this your business, making dolls. I'm so excited for you!

Muffin Cup: I'm ready!

Customers come in and see the dolls standing beautifully on the stands.

Mrs. Thomas: These are beautiful dolls!

Mr. Whitfield: Yes they are, Little Muffin Cup made them.

Mrs. Thomas: She did!? You are only 7 years old, how? Did you have help?

Muffin Cup: No mam!! I took my time and made my way to finish each doll.

Mrs. Thomas: I would like two of them

Muffin Cup: That will be forty dollars even.

Mrs. Thomas: I will give these to my granddaughters for their birthday. Thank you so much.

Muffin Cup: You're welcome.

As Mrs. Thomas goes home and shows off the dolls, word gets spread about the dolls. Now the whole town wants to look at them. Mrs. Thomas carries good news very fast, bragging on this little girls and her dolls.

Mrs. Mary:	Oh my! (with excitement) These are beautiful and you call them "wisdom dolls". This is marvelous. I would like two of them.
Muffin Cup:	Yes mam!

Muffin Cup packed them carefully

Muffin Cup:	Come back soon!
Mr. Whitfield:	Two customers and they only bought dolls.
Mrs. Little:	Well, only an hour went by. Customers will shop for other items. Is there anything Muffin Cup and I could do for you while we wait Mr. Whitfield?
Mr. Whitfield:	No, thank you.
Granny:	This is mighty nice of you letting my little one come here.
Granny:	You are a blessing to her.
Mr. Whitfield:	This is exciting to see this young one make herself famous by using her talent to make these "Wisdom Dolls".

Two more customers come in to buy groceries and to see the dolls. Then others started coming, more and more until soon the store was full. Mr. Whitfield never had his store packed with customers like this before! As the dolls are sold, Mrs. Little and Granny package them up for the customers to take home.

Muffin Cup: I only have five dolls left, what do we do now?

Mr. Whitfield: Well just wait little one and some customers will hear you only have a few left and they will run in here to buy one.

Mr. Whitfield runs to his phone and spread the word about the dolls, telling customers to hurry before they were all gone. Mr. and Mrs. Hurston hurried to the store to get these famous dolls. When they arrived they saw two customers pulling on the last two dolls.

Muffin Cup: Wait, I can make more! Please Stop! If you break, you pay!

Granny: Please Stop! She can make more for whoever wants one, it will be a special order!

Muffin Cup was scared but excited that her dolls sold out and people wanted more!

Muffin Cup: Now calm down ladies. I'm the dollmaker now in one week you will all be able to get what you want. I'm the doll doctor!

After the dolls were gone the couple that came to purchase the famous dolls put in a big order for their store across town.

Granny: I'll take the order and give them to my granddaughter. She is over her head now but she can do it. Mr. Whitfield would like an order also for his store.

Mrs. Little: Well Muffin Cup, now you have to make these dolls and give all your time to make them before school starts. Let's go home, I'm tired now.

On the way home, Muffin Cup counts her money and she is so happy.

Granny: How much did you make?

Muffin Cup: Off thirty dolls, I made $600.00

Mrs. Little: We could make this our company, selling dolls. You just show us how to do it and we could make more.

When they make it home, Corn comes running.

Corn: Hey, how much you make?

Muffin Cup: $600.00!!!

Corn: Six hundred — dollars. Wow!!

Corn: You can buy what ever you want and more supplies.

Muffin Cup: We done good and I have more orders! I will need a prayer on my head to pull this off. This is my gift from God and I'll finish, I know I will!

Granny: You are so true to yourself child.

Corn: Why do you say that Granny we know we tell the truth.

Granny: It's my way of saying things and nothing bad, always a
                 good way of thinking.

Corn: I suppose hanging around Muffin Cup I will talk
                 something old fashioned.

Muffin Cup: I'm sitting on this porch and rest.

Corn: Let's look in a book to see what you want to buy with
                 your money.

Muffin Cup: I don't want to spend this money. I want to just hold on to
                 it for a little while.

Corn: Now you have become a tight wad in thirty minutes. I'm
                 going to ride my bike.

Granny went in the kitchen to make sandwiches, open a bag of chips, and make lemonade.

Granny: Come eat everyone!

At the table eating sandwiches

Granny: The fields are about empty with very little corn left.

Muffin Cup: Well Corn, whatcha gonna do when all the corn is gone?

Corn: We'll sell more of your dolls.

Muffin Cup: You don't seem excited about the corn field being empty.

Corn: I'm tired of corn, the word "corn". I need a break!

Muffin Cup: Out of all the corn you have eaten now you turn your back on it. And plus that corn helped this family make a profit.

Corn: The cornfield is very dear to me not because I love to eat it. We had a lot of fun working together. Next season we will do the same thing, right father?

Mr. Little: Yes we will, and next time it will be much better.

As this story ends, Muffin Cup carries on a good doll making collection and the whole family was famous for corn and making dolls. Everyone in this house helped one another.

Printed in the United States
By Bookmasters

The Centerpiece

of

Love

Pete Frierson

www.trafford.com
North America & international
toll-free: 1 888 232 4444 (USA & Canada)
fax: 812 355 4082

Contents

Love

In Memory of our Loved Ones In God's Heavenly Home

ACKNOWLEDGMENTS

My second book would not have come to fruition so soon without the folks who believed in my ability to share with the world a message of love and happiness through intellectual thoughts.

I am grateful for my team of women—Dollie Butler, Diane Davis, Diane James, and Laura Truelove—who took time out of their lives to share their thoughts, suggestions, and ideas on how to intrigue the hearts, minds, and souls of people who desire to enjoy poetry in a different vein.

My message and dream is to bring people together with love. Without love in our lives, we are often left behind. *The Centerpiece of Love* is intended to bring all emotions within the human heart, mind and soul to a new level of understanding and appreciation for the human race and each other.

The memorials are my way of showing respect and love to those who have gone home to God and a tribute worth noting. It is also my way of reminding all of us that our loved ones continue to be with us as beautiful memories yet never to be forgotten.

Special thanks to the families that allowed me to express my thoughts about their loved ones, as well as my immediate family: my wife, Malinda; my son, Pete Jr.; my daughter, Marteza; my three grandchildren—Sydney, Siraj, and Sanaa; and my daughter-in-law, Alisha.

This book is dedicated to my niece, Porsche Frierson; Kris, Dana, and Jaycie Timms; Roger G. Brown; William E. Duke; Eric L. Harp; James "Heavy" A. Morris and William James and Kerrie Frierson.

I hope that you will enjoy reading *The Centerpiece of Love* and may it soothe your heart, mind and soul.

YOU ARE THE CENTERPIECE OF MY LIFE

You are the centerpiece of my life because you bring me happiness. You change a frown into a smile, a weak heart into a strong one and a laugh into laughter.

You are the centerpiece of my life because, in times of despair, you are there for me. In times of sadness, you bring me joy. In times of doubt, you bring me hope. In times of uncertainty, you give me strength.

You are the centerpiece of my life because, without you, I would be nothing. Without you, I would still be wandering. Without you, there would be no tomorrow.

You are the centerpiece of my life because I can now feel what I could never feel. I can love where I have never loved. You touched me where I could never be touched. I can smile with you in mind. I can do anything because I have you. You are the centerpiece of my life today, tomorrow, and forever, with love.

HAPPY ANNIVERSARY BABY

It's been thirty-nine years and today we celebrate our thirty-ninth year together. A life filled most of the time, with love, faith, respect and understanding, so again I say, "Happy anniversary baby." It was puppy love at first. You were teasing me and I was teasing you. *Bad boy* is the term they use thirty-nine years later. Looking back, those slim long brown tan legs, coupled with those sweet words, probably contributed to me being a bad boy.

As I look back on it, I can say it was the love, respect, faithfulness and the relationship that made us endure, so we now celebrate thirty-nine years of marriage. Happy anniversary baby.

Both of our lives have experienced many transformations. Most of them were all good. Like any marriage, we have to constantly work on it and without a true commitment, we never would have survived the few ups and downs that we experienced.

God forgives us all, even when we are wrong. Neither partner can be right all the time nor can they be wrong all the time. God placed a compromise in the mix, and with Him in our marriage, we can both say "Happy anniversary baby" with a smile. Everything about us has changed. Our feelings, our thoughts, our bodies, our minds, our love and sometimes even our pain, but on this day, we can say, "Happy anniversary baby."

I THOUGHT ABOUT YOU

I thought about you last night, with nothing else to do, as I was sitting in the quietness, reflecting back on life. You appeared on my mind and all of a sudden, I didn't know what to do. I thought about you last night.

I thought about you last night and it carried on through daylight. Today, I am thinking about you. I don't know what it is about you, but last night, I thought about you.

Could it be something we said? Something we did? Maybe the stars aligned themselves in heaven above so that you and I could think about each other as I did last night.

As life would have it, there are some things that cannot be erased. We focus on the good things and we let the bad things go by. No matter how we look at it, I can still say, I thought about you and as the darkness began to set last night, I thought about you.

YOU ARE MY SUNSHINE

You are my sunshine in the morning, at noon and in the evening.
Your smile and laughter are my comfort
when the sun has set.

You are my sunshine at night when my mind is filled with uncertainty.
You are my sunshine when my heart wanders and I think
of your smile and laughter.

You are my sunshine in times of despair when my heart is heavy.
When I let my thoughts drift to my loved ones who have
gone home, you are my sunshine.

As life would have it, there are no dark clouds, uncertain moments,
or a heavy heart when I think of you.
I only see your smile and hear your laughter.

You are my sunshine. I love you for your warmth and your love.
You shall forever be the sun that shines in my life.

WHAT WAS ONCE MINE IS NOW YOURS

What was once mine is now yours—my love is your love, my thoughts are your thoughts, and my dreams are now your dreams.

My world of unknown has come to the light—the light to where you know where I came from and where I am trying to go.
What was once mine is now yours.

The dream of tomorrow and my plan for the future comes to life when I think of you in my world. It is a world that has been hidden
for so many years. I have been afraid to talk about
it in fear of what you might think.

What was once mine is now yours—learn to enjoy the beauty of living,
loving, caring, and sharing. The beauty of just knowing someone
who really loves me. So what was once mine is now yours
to nurture anyway you desire.

Never forget, what was once mine is now yours forever.

I OPENED MY HEART

I opened my heart to the world and now I am afraid.
I am afraid of what might happen and the unknown.

I opened my heart to the world and now I am afraid. I am afraid of
what love might do, what people around me might say and
those that are too afraid to say anything.

I opened my heart to the world and now I am afraid. What if
love comes my way? What am I to do?
Love can be such a wonderful thing when two hearts merge
into one. Shall I open my heart and say,
"I opened my heart and now I am afraid"?

Never be afraid to love. Love makes the heart beat.
Love makes the eyes see.
Love makes the legs run and the mind say,
"I opened my heart and now I am afraid."

Allow me to dream without fear and I know love will make me secure.
I will be secure to return that love from the beginning to end.

I opened my heart to the world and now I am afraid. The words
"I love you too"
resonate in my heart, body and soul forever.
I opened my heart.

NEVER FIGHT THE FEELING

Never fight the feeling of love. Love is a wonderful thing.
It joins the heart, body, mind and soul,
so never fight the feeling.

Age does not make a difference.
When love hits, just sit back and enjoy the pleasure
of what love can do for you.

Never fight the feeling!
I will desire you forever, so never fight
the feeling of love.

IT'S OUR TIME

It's our time to laugh, to smile and to feel totally free.
It's our time to share and love.

It's our time to say no more despair, no more worrying,
no more stressing—just plain and simple fun.

It's our time to plan, to seek and to discover what two people on
the same page can do. It's our time to love,
to share, to touch and to make others wish it was their time.

Sometimes we love from a distance and sometimes we love close.
Sometimes we care from a distance and
sometimes we care close.

Regardless, either way, from a distance or from close, it's our
time to love and to just go with the flow.
It's our time.

CHOICES

We make choices in life. As we begin to grow, we make choices. As we mature into that person that we are going to be, we make more choices and we begin to live with those choices.

Choices, sometimes, may be simple or complicated. No matter how we look at it, we make choices in life. Sometimes though, choices are really hard to decide. Do we choose this or that, or do we move on? Either way, we have choices in life.

Choices are our way of expressing our decisions along the way. Some of us make good choices in life and others make bad choices. Either way, they are choices. As humans, some choices may not be the choice that someone else likes and that choice may not be the right choice, but at that time, it was the choice that you felt was the right choice.

Choices, sometimes, is like playing chess—you don't know whether you are going to make a move or get checkmated. Choices, another part of the human life that we must face, no matter what we do in this world.

Choices are something I want all of you to embrace and do your research before you make a final choice. You do have choices surrounding love, happiness, friendship, companionship, adventure and any other aspect of the human life. Make your choice and live with it. If it is a good choice, smile, smile, and smile. If it is a bad choice, find a way to choose a better one. There is a silver lining in everything that we do. I want you to look for your silver lining and make the right choice because, in life, sometimes that's all we do—make choices.

I KNOW

I know I am not perfect. I know I am not always right.

I know I cannot always understand you.
I know I sometimes run away with things.
I know I can't run and hide forever.

I know I must learn new ways of thinking.
I know I can do whatever is put in front of me.

BUT

I know I can love again. I know I can smile again.
I know I can show you my commitment.
I know we were meant to be for however long.
I know we can grow together.
I know without a doubt.

YOU

are the joy of my life,
the happiness of my soul and the excitement,
yet untold.
Without you in my life somewhere,
I can't go on.
That's how I feel, and that's what I believe.
So I know you are there!

I NEED YOU

Sometimes when we fail to tell someone that we love or care for them so deeply, we miss an opportunity that just may not ever come back again. To need you is to love you. To love you is to need you. To care for you is to show my feelings. To need you is happiness. Happiness is excitement. To touch you is the expression of togetherness.

The need to hold you means closeness and the need to make love to you is our lives joining together to express things God has given us. The need to be with you is the need to say again, "I love you, I need you, I miss you and you are so much a part of my life." You have the touch to bring the best out in me and create memories for a lifetime.

You are my everything. I love you and need you more than I could ever express in words.

I DREAM

I dream of the day that I can look into your eyes and see some joy.
I dream of the day that I can see the smiles and the laughter
of a wonderful person that I know.

I dream of the day that I can hold you, feeling the warmth of
your body and the smell that I love to smell.

I dream of the day that whatever we created will be with us forever.
I dream of the day that we can have some free moments together,
without any drama of any kind from anywhere.

I dream, I dream, I dream that our lives can be joined for whatever
reason, for however long and in the end,
we know the true meaning of love.

I dream of the day that when I am gone and the wind is blowing,
you will be the wind in my heart the wind that's in my soul.
You are the wind that keeps me going.

I dream that we can build something special that only you and I
understand, because it is not for others to understand.

I dream that I will understand someday why my love for you has
been so strong in a world where you have said "We can't."

I dream that one day you will be the center of my life,
my hopes and my dreams. No matter which road I travel, no matter where life takes me,
know that there is one man who loves, cherishes and cares for who you really are.

I dream of the day that we can say we tried it without any regrets.
I dream, I dream, I dream with all my heart, from me to you.

I dream.

I SEE YOU

I see you like no other. I see you when you are happy. I see you when you are sad. I see the passion in you about what life is supposed to be. I see the love that is within your heart and I understand the feeling and the hurt of a broken heart. I see you.

I see you when you don't think that I am looking. I see you out of the corner of my eye. I see you in my heart with all the laughter you deserve. I see you in my soul because I know there could never be anyone else but you. I see you in a different light. I see you.

I see you as someone who is warm, loving, considerate, trusting and very worthy of everything that God would want to take place between a man and a woman. I see you over and over again.

I see the beauty in your face. I see the beauty in your heart and I sense the beauty in your soul. I see the beauty that all others overlook. I see you every day that I am breathing God's fresh air. I realize that the opportunity to love you, to care for you and to be with you is a once in a lifetime opportunity. I see the beauty in you and in me.

I see through the clouds and I find sunshine. I see through the thunderstorms and I bring rain. I see through the cold weather and I bring warmth. I see through the tears and I bring joy. I see through the sadness and despair and I bring happiness. I see you like no other. You are the love of my life and the inspiration in my heart. Without you, I could not see. So on this day, I want you to know that I can see the beauty in you.

I'VE PLAYED THE GAME

I have played the game. Some call it Russian roulette. Others call it a fool's play. The game that I am talking about is not the typical roulette you are thinking of. I am talking about the Russian roulette of *love*.

Russian roulette of love is a dangerous game. It plays with your mind and your heart, not to mention all your emotions. Just when you think that it is going to be all right, suddenly, something goes wrong.

People will tell you anything that you want to hear to get what they want. Women are familiar with this theory because men will say whatever they think a woman might want to hear. Russian roulette of love is not worth it. Only time will tell. Only time will tell the real deal about Russian roulette of love. I have played the game, and I have failed the game. Never play the Russian roulette of love.

WHY DON'T YOU LOVE ME?

A man asked his lady, "Why don't you love me?" and she replied, "I do." But then he said, "Why don't you really love me?" and she could not respond. Then the dialogue begins.

I know the difference between love and real love. Real love is when you feel it all the time and there is no doubt. Love is when you feel something, but that something is missing.

"There is nothing missing," she said, but she could not answer the question of real love. Sometimes we forget the feel of real love or the love that we expressed when we first got together. You know, the kind of love that sent you flowers, candies, gifts, and phone calls. When the feeling of real love is gone, then things begin to change between a man and a woman. It changes and not for the good of the relationship.

Real love is one that you feel when you are happy, sad, lonesome, in bed, driving down the road, or at a sporting event. You know that feeling, you sense that feeling and you look for more reasons to say, "I know real love when I feel it."

So we come back to the question "Why don't you love me?" This can apply to men or women. As you try to understand my logic, allow me to say this: think back to when you were inseparable. What were some of the things that you did. What were some of the things you looked forward to. What were some of the most intimate things you said to each other in order to do what you do as a man or woman?

Now, you can see why real love will keep a relationship strong and love will only make it linger on. Life demands real love, and not puppy love. Stop and think, are you feeling real love at this moment? And if not, stop for a minute and allow your mind to go back to what you did to get him or her. Now, don't you feel the real love that's flowing from your head to your toe? Smile, my friends, just smile. Real love is the only way to go. Real love will make a man or woman want to stay and never let go.

FALSE HOPES

Just when you think you know somebody, things begin to emerge and you see the real person. It can be devastating. We call those false hopes.

Just when you begin to love someone deeply, care for them beyond reproach, emotions begin to flow every which way possible and you are being told this and that, yet nothing ever comes to reality, we call those false hopes.

Just when you begin to trust again, believe in someone, open your heart and let your guard down, then you realize you have been had and you are hurt, so you shut completely down; again, we call those false hopes. Just when life seems on track, something out of the ordinary creeps up. Not sure how to handle it, we reach back into our memory bank, looking for a quick answer, because we know our emotions will turn this event of false hopes into something not pleasant or cause a person to snap.

Regardless of your relationship—father to son, mother to daughter, friend to friend, relative to relative and lover to lover—never play the game of false hopes.

It can turn all the love that you have for one person into something not pleasant. We believe and we want to believe in love and each other. False hopes can turn love into something not pleasant in an instant. Keep love and never play the game of false hopes. That is my message.

MY FIRST IMPRESSION

My first impression of you was a sensation of vibrations of my younger years. The way you carry yourself definitely shows the true meaning of my first impression of you.

My first impression of you was like looking at a queen from the motherland—a queen with so much warmth, kindness, and consideration, with a smile worth a million dollars.

My first impression of you was like diamonds sparkling from afar. Diamonds—when attention is given, polished and displayed—represent what no other stone can do, and that is to show all the loveliness that's inside you. This is my first impression of you.

My first impression of you, I saw that you were quiet, poised, soft-spoken, and attractive, yet very professional from the moment you said "Welcome to . . ." and "May I help you?"

She was once a Northern lady and now she is a Southern lady with that Southern charm. This is my impression of you!

I DON'T WANT TO MISLEAD YOU

I don't want to mislead you because of my kindness and my generosity. I don't want to mislead you because I smile at you, wink at you, or say soft things to your heart. I don't want to mislead you.

I don't want to mislead you when I hug you and I can feel your heartbeat. I don't want to mislead you. I think about all the years that have gone by and it's like we never missed a beat, but today I want you to know that I am not trying to mislead you.

It's not that I have moved on, or it's not that I am staying still; it's just that I am not ready for the next thrill. I am trying to do the things that I know to do. While some nights are lonely, and others are long, I don't want to mislead you.

The years have gone by and my love for you is as strong today as it was years ago, as strange as it may be, I can still feel the warmth, the love and the excitement of yesteryears. As life would have it, it seems as though nothing has changed, but I want you to know that I am not trying to mislead you.

I can't predict the future. I don't know what's in store. It could be as it once was, or it will never be again. Either way, my love for you shall never change. However, I must say to you, with as much love any person can have for another, I don't want to mislead you.

With all my love, I want you to know, again, despite everything in life and everything we have done, memories will be with me until the day that I transcend. I am not trying to mislead you. If the future should compel me to love you like yesteryears, to give you the time like I have before, then so be it. Regardless of the future, I want you to know on this day, I don't want to mislead you.

I CAN'T LOVE A GHOST

I love you—yes, I do! I miss you too and I care for you more than the world knows, but I can't love a ghost. I think about you in the daytime, and at night too, but you are not there. I can't love a ghost.

I see you in my dreams and in my thoughts too. I thought I knew you, but when I touch you, feel you, kiss you, or hug you, you are not there. I can't love a ghost. You are the dream of my life and the center of my thoughts, never having to guess twice just who you are. I can't love a ghost.

Time will pass, the heart will heal and the mind will recover, but my love for the ghost shall never be shattered. I can't love a ghost.

GIVE A WOMAN SOMETHING AND SHE WILL GIVE MORE

"Give a woman something, and she will give more" is a phrase that has such deep meaning, but as men, we must give from the heart because, when we give from the heart, it is received to her heart and it multiplies.

Sometimes when we fail to give a woman something, we get nothing in return and we ask ourselves why. No matter who you are, that line could apply to you. Of course, there is a lady out there somewhere who would say, "Give a man something and he will give you more," and I don't doubt that, but we know this is a woman's world and we have to learn to get along.

"Give a woman something and she will give more" can be a blessing to some folks because sometimes a woman has received so little in life that she is so appreciative of whatever a man does.

Shower her with flowers, love, adventures, surprises, trust, understanding, and a commitment to just her, and she will give you more. Simply put, give a woman something, and she will give you more.

To the men out there, that beautiful rose was somebody's daughter and she could still be. Never forget, someday, you may have a daughter and you will want someone to be nice to her and to give her something so that she can give more.

THE RACE OF LIFE

The race of life is like starting from point A—we run, we run and we run. Sometimes, we have to stop after we have run for so long and so far. The race of life tires you out. We just have to keep on keeping on.

The race of life can be like a tornado. It comes quick, fast and in a hurry. Issues attack us from out of nowhere. We call this the race of life.

When we think everything is all right and everything appears to be rosy, then trouble comes from out of nowhere. We call this the race of life.

For those of us who don't run, don't hide and don't blame others, we take responsibility and do whatever we need to do. At the end of the day, we call this the race of life.

The race of life can be precious. It can be some of the most joyous moments in life. The race of life can be like no other. The good Lord lets us wake up each morning and breathe His fresh air all day long. That is even called the race of life.

The race of life is like no other. It brings happiness to your face, a smile to the heart and joy to the body. It uplifts the spirit and sometimes it brings all the opposite. We call this the race of life.

We could run and we could hide. We could blame others. That too is called the race of life. But you can only run for so long, hide for so long and you can only blame others for so long. Then it comes to an end and we can no longer call it the race of life.

When you start out the gate with your mind so focused, you know without a doubt, that whatever you do that day is going to be called the race of life. Whether we run a mile, walk five minutes, jog all day long, chitchat to others and text like no other, and when the day is over, we still call it the race of life.

No matter how you look at this and no matter what you think, we call this the race of life. So I say, run with joy, smile with joy and jump with joy. Let no one steal your joy. At the end of the day, we call this the race of life.

I'M SORRY FOR WHAT I DID TO YOU

I'm sorry for what I did to you when you were so good to me. In the end, I failed to see the value of our friendship, our love and our companionship. I'm sorry for what I did to you when I was down and out. You were there for me when I had no one to turn to; you were there for me.

I'm sorry for what I did to you—listening to others who I thought, in my weakest moments, would uplift me and give me courage to carry on. I was wrong! I'm sorry for what I did to you. The pain, your sleepless nights, the tension, the confusion and everything else in between—I'm sorry for what I did to you.

If I could do it all over again, it would be different. I can see now, I can listen now, I can communicate now and I can understand your thoughts and see life in a new light.

While I can't change yesterday, I can truly say, "I'm sorry for what I did to you." Forgive me, as my God would do.

STELLA

Somewhere, my best friend Stella, is out there protecting those who need protecting. Standing tall for those not so tall, defending right from wrong, and punishing those who need to be punished. My friend is somewhere out there, doing what needs to be done.

Sometimes the wrong cannot see or understand my best friend's tough stand against those who disrespect the laws of our land. Sometimes, but rare, my best friend will give someone another chance to change their life and to change their ways, but remember, my best friend believes in and stands for what's right and not what's wrong!

My friend is somewhere out there. Over two decades ago, we became best friends and time has not separated our friendship. We had a task to do and we did it well!

My best friend is somewhere out there and I know where to find my best friend. Stand tall, my friend and justice will always reveal itself to you until the very end. You will always and forever be my best judicial or, otherwise, friend for life. Friends forever. Stand tall, Stella. Stand tall.

THE DAY I MET ERIK

Today I met a young man named Erik
who loves Corvettes, 'Vettes for short.
He admires Corvettes. He smiled,
he laughed and he talked about his love
for Corvettes.

Today I met a young man named Erik. He once
toured the Corvette plant and they gave
him a ride. He was admiring and laughing
all the way. Wow! To his delight, his face
shined with joy, just being driven around in
a Corvette.

I gave him a T-shirt and he admired my
'Vette too. It was the thrill of his lifetime
and a joy in my heart to share such a special
moment with a very special young man named Erik.

Written for Erik, who loves Corvettes and I love them too.

TO MY EXPECTING FRIEND

God has blessed you with the chance to have a baby girl.

Babies are dear, sweet, loving, caring, and yes, they cry, want to be fed and want to be dry, so get ready my expecting friend.

Party days have come and gone. Now you will have a new friend, one that you help create with the Lord's help. So get ready my expecting friend.

I remember when you were so small and now I have seen your transformation. You still look and act like you are small, except when you wobble like a duck. So get ready my friend.

I see in your face the joy that you and your husband have joyously created. People in this world wish for your expecting joy, but God blessed you. So to my expecting friend, do all those things necessary to help bring your bundle of joy into this world as healthy as can be.

So to my expecting friend, get ready, be ready, enjoy your expected bundle of joy and I wish you and yours the best.

Patience my dear. It will soon be all over and when it's over, you can say, "What a joy . . . what a joy . . . thank God it's over, but what a bundle of joy."

Have fun and enjoy your beautiful expecting friend. Thank God for your beautiful baby girl named Olivia.

MY DAUGHTER

My daughter is my heart, born on the day Martin Luther King left this world. I knew I had a fighter. It's known that I love my daughter with all my heart. I will stand by her and I am her rock, no matter what. In her lifetime, I can say we have only disagreed twice on things that caused a conflict. As life would have it, we worked out our differences and now we agree to disagree.

A daddy's love is different for a girl than the one for a boy. Either way, there is love. Her middle name stands for love. The love of the human race, the love of family, the love of Mom and Dad, the love for a big brother and the love that remains unspoken. Quiet in nature, that she is, but I can tell you, she has the fight of Martin and Malcolm too. She took that part from her daddy, who taught her to believe in something and stand for what she believed in.

A daddy's love for his daughter cannot be matched by anything in this world. We live to see our children grow up to become whatever their heart desires and we support them the best way we can. We never forsake a day, week, month or even years because we can never turn back the hands of time.

I am proud to have a daughter like I do and I will tell the world that I will stand by and with her. I know what my role is in life toward her and I will never forget that I had a hand in bringing her into this old world too. She is my angel and my star. She has never caused me to take the walk of shame and I know deep down inside that she never will.

So when the time comes and I am gone, she will remember the things we have done. Tene' will know that I loved her with all my heart—the man who taught her right from wrong—her father, her daddy.

NEVER GIVE UP

Never give up no matter what. Even at your weakest moment in life and you think that there is nothing else for you to do but roll over and say, "Lord, come get me," never give up.

Never give up because giving up is not the solution. I can understand when the body is tired, when you have endured and then when you can't endure anymore, I understand those who may want to say, "I am ready to see my Maker." But on the other hand, as life would have it, we are going to have many ups and downs, many trials, many tribulations, and many sleepless nights. But never give up.

Always have a positive mind and a positive insight into life, no matter what the situations may be; you too will see what I have seen and you never give up.

My writings may sometimes reflect the pain that I have endured for over twenty-plus years, and there have been times when I have wanted to say, "Lord, take me," but I decided that I will never ever give up.

No matter what my situation may be—physically, mentally, emotionally, financially, spiritually and any other way that you chose to look at life—never give up.

The day that I decided to focus on me and not everything around me—including friends, family, children, work, social life and so forth—my life began to change.

ROGE (MY BEST FRIEND)

You are my best friend; we go back years and years. The day is going to come that all I can do is reminisce about all the things that you and I have done. You are my best friend.

I remember all the things that we used to do. Some were good and some were not so good. But we made a promise to each other that we would be friends until the end. We shared things that we have done, good or bad. You are my best friend.

So the question to some may be, "What is a best friend?" The answer is simple: a best friend is someone who will be there with you to the end no matter the situation, time of day or time of night—your best friend will be there.

A best friend is someone who will drop everything that they are doing to be at your bedside, if that is the situation. A best friend knows what you think, what you like and what you want, more so than others. You are my best friend and you will be my best friend until the end.

Sometimes life's situation and distance can cause the fiber to stretch between two best friends, but the fiber shall never break. I say to you, if you have a best friend and you only need one, keep that friend until the end. In today's world, if people can't write, can't call, or can't send a card, then just send a text and say, "You are my best friend."

LISTEN TO THE RAIN

Listen to the rain. It dances with each raindrop. Sometimes a fast-moving dance, sometimes a slow-moving dance, and other times it seems to be rapping. Listen to the rain. It will give you such a fresh feeling.

Listen to the rain. It soothes the soul, excites the heart and refreshes the brain. Wow, what a feeling to listen to the rain dance and feel the smell of fresh rain.

Listen to the rain. Sometimes it comes with a slow start, sometimes with a roar, and other times with enough force to make you want to dance. The sound of rain soothes the soul and relaxes the mind and if you are careful, it will rest and refresh the brain. Listen to the rain.

Listen to the rain, and beware of the roar. Sometimes it comes with a thunder and other times it comes with dark clouds and bright lights called lightning. Just listen to the rain and it will soothe your soul, relax the mind and refresh the brain. Listen to the rain.

EXPAND YOUR MIND

The good Lord gave all of us the ability to think and reason. There comes a time that we must learn to expand our minds. Don't be afraid to take on a new challenge. It makes life worth living.

Expand your mind and relax. You will discover the many wonders that life has to offer. The mind will play tricks on you to see if you are paying attention. Stand firm in your quest to be the best and let nothing stop you in achieving what life has in store for you.

Expand your mind and see the world. Expand your mind to want to do things that you never thought you could do. Make things happen. Make all our dreams come true.

Expand your mind to new heights. Go where you thought you could never go and see the beauty of the world. Meet the people that God created and enjoy each day as if it was your last one.

Expand your mind, open your eyes, dream again, create new things and plan ahead for tomorrow. I know you have the ability to do whatever is in your heart. Expand your mind, and renew life like never before for God is with you every step of the way. Expand your mind and live.

WHY I CAN'T QUIT

Sometimes life seems so hard with the many challenges that affect the body and mind, but I continue to move on. I can't quit when faced with uncertainty, because that is not in my DNA.

The road is rough to travel and the hills are even worse, yet I know I can't quit. There are folks like you that care and folks like you that share a common bond of "I can't quit."

I live in a world where despite everything, I can't quit. Sometimes the mind tries to make me think I need to give up, but I know I can't quit. Life is too good as even in the midst of everything that's happening around you, God is always there. Believing in Him will make tough matters seem so small and lighter matters seem like nothing at all. I can't quit.

The sun shines when least expected and good things happen on the same accord. You begin to smile again. You begin to live again and just for those two reasons alone, I can't quit.

Born to enjoy life for whatever it is worth, I must go on. Knowing one day that I must transcend from this life to the other side, I must carry on to the end. I can't quit.

MY INSPIRATION

You are my inspiration—north, south, east, and west. Without you in my life, I am lost. Wandering in a world of uncertainty, you are my inspiration because you inspire a new life within me. You give me the sparkle to smile. You are my inspiration.

You are my inspiration because God gave me you. You are such a warm delightful inspiration. You are my inspiration because of your touch, your smile, the look in your eyes and the way you take time out of your life to show me my weakness, but at the same time, you inspire me to new heights.

My life changed the day we decided to be on the same page, realizing what we could or could not do. You inspire me to want to live again, to live a full life and to enjoy each day with the inspiration of you in my heart, body and soul.

A gift from God—you are not realizing even today why He sent you my way. I cannot question what has happened, but I can follow your inspirations no matter where they take me.

You are my inspiration for life and on this day, I want you to know there will always be love for you from me. Inspiration of life and inspiration of love, that's what you are to me.

MY FRIENDS

Old friends never die. They are like the oceans that flows and flows and memories will always be told. There were other friendships along the way, but only a few withstood time and the ways of life.

As life would have it, along the way, I met some special friends and special friends are worth more than a million in gold. Roger was my friend growing up and we stayed close until our military duty called us and then distance became a way of life.

William and I joined the navy under the Buddy Program and we were buddies throughout boot camp and military school and then our military orders separated us. He followed in my footsteps as a true gold winger.

Eric came along during my tour in the Philippines and even today we remain friends. Somehow distance has separated us, but the bond between old friends remains strong.

Finally, I want to share my story about James. Today, James has a medical condition that does not allow him to remember much and it hurts to just wonder what he is thinking in his mind, but he can't say it. Distance seemed so far until I learned that he had fallen ill and then no distance could stop me from seeing him.

I drove down to Pensacola to see my friend and hear the ocean roar. Hidden in between was the Pensacola Bay. It reminded me of all the good times that James and I used to have as young sailors and now we can only wait and pray that a miracle will come his way and I will once again see my friend the way that I have always known him. He was just full of fun. Just full of fun. I shall return soon to see my friend.

I LOVE ME SOME BOO

She loved her some Boo. He was good to her. The first time she laid eyes on him, she knew she was in love. The times they spent together were times never to be forgotten. She loved her some Boo.

He was a warm kind and a gentleman. Forever caring he was to a woman who just found her first love. They kissed, they planned and they did things, but time got away and their paths changed. But years later, they would reconnect and once again, she said, "I love me some Boo."

It was the most enjoyable time of her life, proud to announce to the world that she and her Boo were back together again. Mom was full of happiness for her daughter. Those years that flew by were years that she would never get back. She was determined not to lose her Boo again.

She did her best to keep him, but life had other plans. His time on earth would end, but it was known that his little brother would find his love and tell her the sad news that he was gone. Life would have it that she called his phone on the day he was to leave this world. He recognized her voice and said, "I love you" and "Take care." Those were his last words to the woman he loved.

Today, she still thinks about her Boo and often she cries, but deep down in her heart, she knows there was only one Boo. He loved her with all his heart. Rest in peace, my brother, rest in peace.

LADY MEL

Lady Mel is her name, sweet as can be, raised in the state, two cousins to Tennessee, depending on which way you travel. Nevertheless, Lady Mel is a lady of few words, but those few words have more meaning than most, spoken from a woman who is wise and knowledgeable.

Lady Mel is my girl. From the day I knocked on her door as a stranger, she has been my friend and my best friend.

Lady Mel always has something good to say about someone. She spends her time thinking about this or that, wondering what she can do next.

Even past eighty, she smiles, she laughs and she tells jokes, but she also speaks her mind. That's Lady Mel, one of a kind!—friendly, charming and loving. My Lady Mel.

Don't let it be said that she does not care about family, friends, neighbors and strangers. You would be wrong. She's always out there lending a hand.

Lady Mel, I love you for who you are and all the things you continue to do. Even if you are two cousins to Tennessee, depending on which way you travel. Love, the son you never birthed.

I NEVER STOPPED LOVING YOU

I never stopped loving you from the day that I laid eyes on you. I could never forget your beautiful eyes, your beautiful smile and the way you presented yourself.

I never stopped loving you because I felt I could always love you no matter what. In the end, my beliefs became a reality. I never stopped loving you.

I never stopped loving you even when sunny days became cloudy or when cloudy days became rainstorms or when rainstorms became thunderstorms. Through it all, I never stopped loving you.

I never stopped loving you when something seemed to creep into your mind. I never walked away in the beginning, in the middle, or in the end of a crisis. I always stayed there to the bitter end because I never stopped loving you.

I never stopped loving you when your laughter could be felt a thousand miles away, it seemed, or when your smile could make a person feel new again. I never stopped loving you when we took walks in the park and we held hands or we took a moment out to swing. I never stopped loving you in the midst of turmoil or in the middle of joy. I never stopped loving you.

I never stopped loving you when the body seemed to be breaking down and you needed a little help. I was there to run your errands, to do your chores, to hold your hand, to read with you and to make jokes with you. All those things were necessary to show you why I stayed because I never stopped loving you.

I never stopped loving you because I knew in my heart of hearts and in my mind of minds that you were one beautiful person. Sometimes they call them a diamond in the rough that only needed a little cultivating, nurturing and respect. I gave all those things, and I never stopped loving you.

When I lie down at night and I think of you, my mind runs a hundred miles an hour thinking about this, that, and the other. I think about things that we did in the past. Most of all, my mind always lets me look to the future. As I look out into the future, I still see that beautiful, warm and loving person that I will never stop loving.

Months have turned into years and years have turned into decades. Not every day has been a rose garden, but there are days that we could use to continue to build and build and build because the foundation of love, happiness and togetherness was all made into one. Even today as you read this, you will see and feel the love that I have for you. That's why I can say today, I have never stopped loving you.

I have never stopped loving you because there was no other love like yours. There was no other person in the world like you. There was no one else that could make my heart flutter, make my eyes blink uncontrollably and make my blood flow faster than the Mississippi River and still be able to give me that sense of belonging. I want you to know today as I say to the world no matter what time, place, or day, "I never stopped loving you."

DODGE CITY

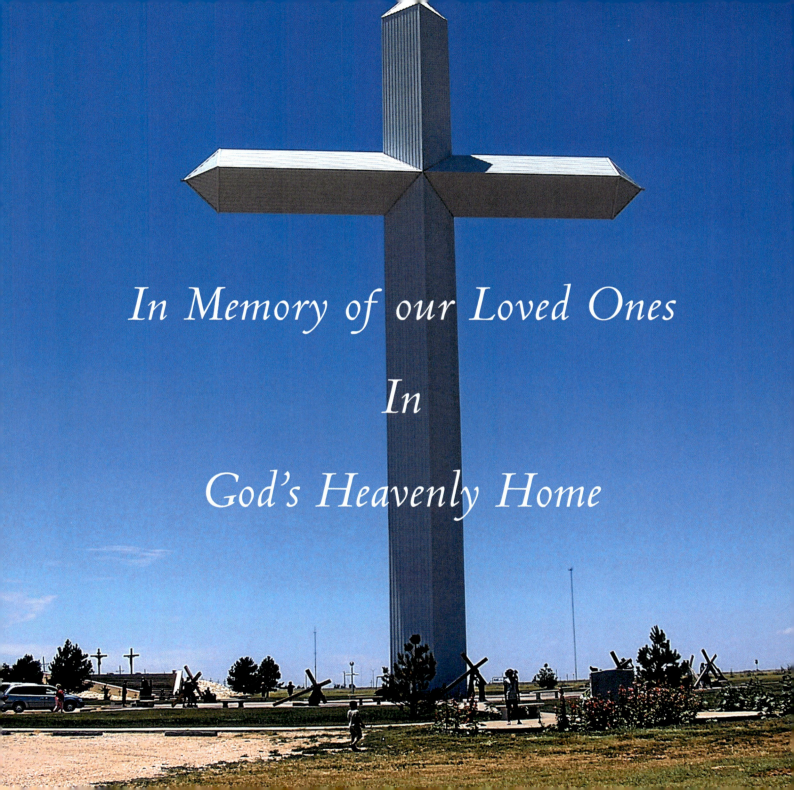

In Memory of our Loved Ones

In

God's Heavenly Home

OUR MOTHER AND OUR FATHER

Mothers are very special and fathers are too. Sometimes we find ourselves closer to one than the other. In my life, I had both parents, but my mother influenced me the most.

It's not a day that goes by that we don't think about our mother and the things that she taught us and how well she did to make us who we are.

Our father was a hard worker and he worked very hard for all of us. I believe he was trying to teach us the meaning of hard work and to show us how to get what we wanted out of life the hard way yet expressing the easy way through education.

Our mother was very sweet and gentle to everyone that she encountered, regardless of their situation in life. I admired our mother for having such a warm, loving and trusting heart.

She was a wonderful woman and she had a wonderful personality. I know our mother and father is with God. They are in heaven, dancing on the street paved with gold. Our day shall come when we will join our parents in heaven. Oh, what a day that will be, no more tears and no more pain.

Our father loved a little bit of politics and he enjoyed that to the very end. He also had a heart that was warm and loving. He would give you the shirt off his back if he thought you truly needed it. He was the best father that we could have had and he did the best that he could with what he had.

My sister and I were at the ER when he left this world and his last words were, "Doctor, Doctor, I want to go home now," and the doctor replied, "As soon as we get the results of your test." Our father then repeated those words, took three breaths and went home to God.

In memory of our loving parents, God giveth and God taketh away. All of us still miss them deeply. We know they are still enjoying life, just not on this side.

Our last words: There is not a day gone by without a single sigh. There is not a day gone by that you are not thought about. There is not a day gone by that we do not feel your love. There is not a day gone by when we feel that you are still there. There is not a day gone by that something you said, something you did, or something you meant for us to remember does not cross our minds. Just looking in the mirror each day is our daily reminder of you. Mom and Dad, this is to you, with love, from all your children, grandchildren and all the rest of us. Rest in peace.

MOMMA BETTY

Mom is not gone. She has gone home to God's kingdom.

Betty, your gentle giant, Dewey, went home first to prepare for his queen and now you are on your way. What a reunion that will be!

She was soft-spoken, kind, considerate, well-respected and now her wings are on cruise control headed to meet her gentle giant.

Mom, you are not gone. You are in God's kingdom, the kingdom in the sky, where Mom shall never fear, never cry and never have another pain. That's the kingdom in the sky.

GOOD-BYE, GENTLE GIANT

Your day has come and gone, but your legacy shall live on. Many of your friends, relatives and loved ones have expressed their love openly and publicly for a gentle giant with a heart of a king and passion of many men.

Your day has come and gone, so to my friend Dewey, you always knew how to do things your way. So on this day, it is snowing, white and wet. We can't move, we can't leave, and it's snowing in Detroit.

The wind is blowing north, south, east, and west, with snow falling upon my face. Nose red and wet, it is snowing in Detroit.

Here to pay my respects to a gentle giant, a man I came to respect the first day we met.

He is not gone. He is like a snowflake that glitters like gold. My friend Dewey is still glittering like gold on this day.

So to the gentle giant, it's snowing in Detroit, white as it can be. He's gone home to take his rest. He departed this earth peacefully. So as he is laid to rest, Kenwood Dewey Turner, all I can say is, "What a beautiful day to celebrate your home-going."

Like doves, it is snowing in Detroit. Good-bye, my friend. It was an honor to have known you and to have you as my friend.

Good-bye, gentle giant, good-bye. Your day has come and gone and your legacy shall live on. You and Mama Betty are now joined again. Live on, my friend, live on.

J.B. AND HATTIE MAI

The years have gone by and you are not forgotten. I can recall the day I married your daughter and the many years that followed. God allowed me the opportunity to become a part of the Johnson family. As God took J.B. from us, those memories still remain. Many years after he left this side, Ms. Hattie continued the warm and loving spirit with me as she did from the first time I met her.

God makes no mistakes. Ms. Hattie was one of a kind. To this day, I remember the day she was called home. There are things that were named after her, like a van that we called 1204. That van seemed to never quit. We can recall all the things that we have done with our loved ones, and she is no exception.

While J.B. and Ms. Hattie are no longer with us on this side, their spirit, love, and compassion still remain. We are grateful for the time that God allowed us to be with them and to cherish every moment while they were on earth.

You will never be forgotten and we think about you often. Like the April showers and May flowers, you are there. May the love you shared with us remain forever. Your son-in-law.

MY NEIGHBOR, MY FRIEND, MY MOTHER

My neighbor, my friend and my mother, Ruby Bobo has gone home and I was not there to say good-bye; but I am there in spirit and you are in my heart.

To my neighbor, my friend and my mother, Mrs. Bobo, you were my neighbor and Lord knows you and Sherman were the best ever! You were my friend next, and what a friend and neighbor you were. I can recall so many days we chatted about this and that. Someone who was always ready to give a helping hand no matter what.

You became my mother in October 1985. My mom left for heaven April 25, 1985, and Mrs. Bobo stepped in. She loved me like I was one of her own. She was always including me and my family in family activities and much more.

She was a mother to me, just like she was a mother to her own children. She was a person with a warm and loving heart. She cared about family.

To the family, our mom is not gone. She is resting and rejoicing with the Lord. So let your heart be at peace and thank God for her life. She lived it well.

BOBBY "PETERBILT" BOBO

Bobby, as life would have it, you left us suddenly. Without any warnings, you were gone. Like an eagle, you flew away to heaven.

Bobby, your laughter, your smile, your tender heart, your sense of humor, your wisdom and your love shall live on through the hearts of many.

Bobby, you always did things your way and you did it to the very end. There will never be another Bobby Ray Bobo like you. Some of us will try to act like you, have fun like you, think like you and hug like you, but we can never be you.

You have gone home and you will be missed deeply on this side, but with our faith we will see you on the other side.

You were a rock to so many and even though you are gone, the family will remain rock solid.

Say hello to all our loved ones in heaven: Mama, Daddy and all the rest.

REMEMBRANCE OF MOTHER

My mother has gone home to God. He opened His hands and He called her home to be in the kingdom. Mother is gone, but her love lives on—the joy of her voice, the tenderness of her touch, the happiness of her smile and the tenderness of her love. My mother is gone, but her memories live on! I may cry a tear here or there, but it is a tear of joy. It is a tear of happiness that says, "Mom is gone, yet her precious memories lives on."

God's hands opened up as wide as can be. Come on in, my child, because this is the kingdom for you and me. Mom lives on! Don't cry, my child. Mom is not gone.

I am with my God and happy as can be. Don't cry, my child, because I am not gone. I am the wind that blows, the sun that shines, the clouds that cover the sky and the snow that glows like the heavens above. So again, my child, do not cry because I am not gone! I am in heaven with my God. Don't cry, my child, not even a tear.

My motherly love will surround you today, tomorrow and forever. This is the love of your mother and it will be there during the day or the night. Don't cry, my child. Just smile because I am in the heavens with God, with no tears and nothing but my love for you, my dear.

MY BROTHER, MY FRIEND

Clarence was my brother first and my friend second; mixed together, we were inseparable. Many days, many nights and thousands of miles we spent together traveling, especially the Western parts of the United States.

My brother, my friend, in September 2011, you wanted to go West, and we did. We stopped in St. Louis, Missouri, to see his daughter, Darrolyn. He wanted to go visit Anheuser Bush Beer Brewery and we did . . .

We wore him out, but he sipped and sipped on a Bud until we got our buzz on and only an ounce did it for the both of us.

Darrolyn instantly became the designated driver. Sadly for us, she drove like a bat out of hell hitting every pothole in St. Louis. When we finally arrived back at home, she said, "Uncle Pete, why don't you give me this car?" It wasn't much left after surviving all those potholes. The buzz was gone by the time we got home.

It was fun and enjoyable for my brother and my friend. I will miss him more than anyone will know, with the exception of a few.

As life was coming to an end, he had placed a meat order with our brother and friend in Colorado, E. James.

Clarence called him and said, "Pete and I will be there June 1st and I want elk, deer, buffalo meat and a fat goat . . . And please, no mountain lion." That order was filled. Two days before he left this world, he said, "I am going to get better and we are going to Colorado, June 1st."

God canceled that order for him and filled another. He said, "I believe, Clarence, that you have endured and endured, it's time to come home." My brother, my friend, you left me. Lord willing I will be in Colorado on June 1st and I will keep my promise. Your resting place will be those beautiful mountains of Colorado. You will fly like an eagle, smiling all the way down, saying, "Run, deer, run. Run, elk, run. Swim, fish, swim." And out through the sunset, you shall go. My brother, my friend.

My healing may take longer than most, but I will heal for us. Your words will be forever in my mind and my heart. Your sense of humor and bluntness will remind me of just who you were. The memories will last a lifetime. Your smile will be like sunshine, and those that you have touched can recall the good old days of what you did and what you knew better not to do. He did it his way.

You have broken the chain of the Frierson's clan, but the chain will mend. In death, you have done what you could not do while you lived. Through you, slowly but surely, you will see from above as we come together to finish the reunion that we started when our late mother left this world twenty-six years ago. In death brother, the force of you, Father, and Mother are doing what life didn't give you the true chance to do! Twenty-six years later, brother, you have your reunion. May the next one not be because of death.

Today brother, we celebrate your life. Forgive me brother, for having this memorial service. I know I went against your wishes but, brother there are many who love you, many who respected you and many who just wanted to say good-bye.

As tough as I may seem, my love for you will not allow me not to cry. My tears are of joy and not sorrow. You are where there are no more tears and no more pain.

As I close, just a couple more things. This gathering and the words of many show the love we all have for you.

We love you and good-bye, my brother. Good-bye, my friend. In 124 days, I shall let you fly like an eagle and hear you say, "Run, deer, run . . . run, elk, run . . . swim, fish, swim . . ."

Good-bye, brother. With love, your little brother.

January 28, 2012

Baxter Brothers Chapel

Columbia, Tennessee

MONEY RUNNER

This is not his given name by any means. Money Runner is a name given to him as a professional truck driver. He traveled over a million miles and he saw the world from a different prospective. He met many people along the way and he welcomed them with a smile.

Money Runner, you have gone home now, and while you left this world, there are many of us who are still here. We think about you often because you are still so fresh and so dear in our hearts. You fought a hard battle and finally you said that you have had enough and you were ready to go home. We were not ready for you to leave, but that was between you and your God. Money Runner is the man with a big heart.

Money Runner, there are a lot of folks who did not understand you. It was not meant for them to understand you. You had your own uniqueness about things that you chose to do. You chose those that you wanted to be near you. You are missed today. You are thought about more often than you can imagine and it is because of how you carried yourself.

I am sure that the day that we said good-bye, you were watching, and the day that we spreaded your ashes over the canyon, as you had asked, down the canyons you went and up you came back. We repeated that scenario several times before you finally said, "I am ready" and "Good-bye, let me go."

IN MEMORY OF ROOSEVELT JONES

THE ONE LEFT BEHIND

My time on earth has ended. Only God knows why he took me so suddenly. Don't ask why because there is no real answer except God knows best. Perhaps my time seemed all too brief, but don't lengthen it now with undue grief. Lift up your hearts and share it with me. God wanted me now. He set me free.

I can't say it does not hurt because I left so suddenly, but just remember all the memories of me and your heart, will be set free.

To the ones I left behind, you shall see me again in God's heavenly hands. Share our memories of all the laughter, the fun, the travel and the many burnouts I did. Now, I am where burnouts are like gold and with each burnout, it healed my soul.

My sudden departure was not my choice. It was God's doing, not mine. Dry the tears, open your heart and remember that memories are forever. To the ones I suddenly left behind. In memory of Roosevelt Jones.

SO WHEN THIS LIFE IS OVER WE MUST GO ON

ROOSEVELT

When this life is over on this side of the world, those left behind must live on. We cannot spend an hour, a day, a week, a month or a year trying to figure out why because there is no answer and God knew best.

When this life is over, those left behind must live on. I am one of those who was left behind and now let's refocus our hearts, our minds, and our souls to march forward with our heads held high and with a beautiful smile that would warm the heart of anyone who would look into God's beautiful eyes.

I can no longer cry because I have cried all my tears. I can no longer live as if though Roosevelt is still here. We can go visit his resting place, but he is not there. He has gone home to where there are no worries and no more pain.

You have to carry on because you are the ones who were left behind. No one can say it does not hurt to lose a loved one, because it does, but it is the memories that we built together on this earth and it is the memories that will carry us on when you are the one left behind.

IN MEMORY OF MY HUSBAND, JD

JD, I remember when we got married, we took a vow to say that in times of sickness, we would be there for each other. JD darling, I know you are not physically with me, but my love still grows in my heart, my mind and my spirit. I am thankful for your last smile and your last words before you flew with the angels to heaven and you said, "I cannot live with this pain."

I understand that pain today because you are gone and like the Indians would say, "I have to let you go too," so that our spirit can be at peace. Then, I can do what I think you would want me to do, and that is to find peace and happiness.

JD, I thank you for preparing me for the day you left this old world. Thank you for your love, inspirations, insights and the gentleness of your touch and your words that I would be all right. He prepared me to become stronger and not weaker, so I would be able to stand on my two feet and not on weak legs. He prepared me to face tomorrow with my head up and with a smile on my face.

JD, as much as I am lost, I am trying to keep you alive. Knowing you are with the angels gives me new life. Today shall be the beginning of a new life for me because I can feel that the burden I have carried so long has been lifted from my heart.

The good Lord said, "I will only put upon you as much as you can bear," and I have reached that point. I know my husband is with God in heaven—a place where there are no more tears and no more pain, where the streets are paved of gold. I know one day I will go to that mansion in heaven and I shall rejoin my JD; Your loving wife LD.

THE CIRCLE OF LIFE

The circle of life is an important part of living and dying. We live to become one and we live to try to do the right things as we have been taught. Sometimes, we get off track with what we are taught and it can cause much, much pain. But the circle of life will lift your burdens, I promise you. See, the circle of life begins at birth. We grow up to love and to find love and sometimes find a mate and hope to live happily from now on. The circle of life brings back the love and the memories of our dear loved ones.

Sometimes, we wish we could have another moment with them; and sometimes that opportunity is given, and other times it is not. Don't beat yourself up because you didn't get the chance to say one last thing before God took our loved ones away from us.

The circle of life brings back that love and memories over and over again. Say to yourself "While I missed that last opportunity to say good-bye, God will give me another chance to say good-bye" or "I will see my loved ones in heaven." You are never wrong when you trust and believe in the Lord.

Sometimes, if we could just say to them, "I love you, and I understood the cloth that you were made from," things would seem better within our hearts, and as I write this, your heart rejoices from just reading these words: "she knew my heart." Let me share with you again, they already knew your heart and God knew your heart too. Take a deep breath and enjoy the circle of life with those who have gone home, just knowing that they knew your heart is all that really matters.

WHEN WE LOSE A LOVED ONE

When we lose a loved one, the emotions run very deep. Sometimes it brings with it a broken heart. When we lose a loved one, we try our best to keep it together. Sometimes we can, and sometimes we can't.

When we lose a loved one, we think about all the things we said, the things that we have done and for some of us, we think about all the things that we meant to do, could have done and just wouldn't. But it's too late now.

When we lose a loved one that doesn't mean that we have lost that person entirely. It means that the good Lord has carried them home to that beautiful place in the sky.

When we lose a loved one, especially suddenly, it hurts because the human mind can adjust to what's happening, even though we may not be ready to let go. Sometimes, we don't understand why and it is my belief that it is not meant for us to. I think God sometimes gives us a test and that test is trusting in his word, his teachings, and his love. Nevertheless, when we lose a loved one, it hurts, plain and simple.

When we lose a loved one, we think about all the memories that we created and there will be many, many, many stories told about our loved ones from a child to a teenager, to an adult and to the end of life. Your memory and your love did not die. It lives on and on in the hearts of many.

When we lose a loved one, sometimes we try to mend a broken heart and it works and sometimes a broken heart does not mend. I have seen it in my lifetime. Either way, I say to you, when you lose a loved one, think about the memories, think about the good times, think about things you did that no one else dared to do think about things that you promised yourself that you would do and with that you will walk away saying to yourself, "My loved one is gone, but their memories and I still live on." When you lose a loved one, just remember the love.

IN MEMORY OF SUSAN KINSER

Susan, you are gone, but not forgotten. The many good deeds that you performed while here on earth shall live on in the hearts of many. I remember your pleasant smile as we talked about Mr. Parker, the ghost and your excitement of what might lie between those walls.

I remember your kindness and your concern for everyone that you came in contact with and that showed the person that you were.

I can never forget the day you and your sister, Cindy, left me as neighbors and co-tenants, but those memories are there forever.

As you transcend into heaven, I leave these words for your loved ones to remember and reflect upon as they think of you. "When someone you love becomes a memory, that memory becomes a treasure." For me and the mass of people who knew you, let her memory become your memory, let her guide to God become our guide and let her shining light become our shining light of the life she lived.

Her love lives in all of us. Good-bye, my friend, good-bye.

DRAKE, OUR FRIEND

In the morning, in the afternoon,
late in the evening, you cross our minds.
I'm told you are gone, but when the
sun rises, when the sun sets and moon glows,
your smiling face still shows.

Years come and years go.
Memories fade and memories glow.
Some stories told and some will never unfold.

Tenderhearted as you were, gentle as could be,
you left us behind to face another day.

Some wept, some cried, some shared stories
and others are still untold.
Those you served will never go away.
Your smile, your personality,
your kindness will often be told.

The day will come and we all can say,
"Drake, the day has come for you to rise,
rise like the sun, the moon and the stars."

MR. CATHEY

His name to most was Timothy, but for me it was Mr. Cathey. A charming character he was, always full of fun. Never a day would go by that he didn't stop in to check on his friend, Mr. Frierson.

There were days that I wanted to toss him out for his loudness and not his charm. He would cool down and then ask, "Man, can you give me a drink or a dollar?" Sometimes I would do just that in order to convince him to leave and other times I would just walk away with a smile.

Why? It was because my friend, on some occasions, had a little too much to drink. Either way, he was my friend. He would make you laugh, get loud and wanted to play like two kids. I will never forget my friend.

He will be missed by many—those that knew he was conning them out of this and that. The others he charmed like a slick cat. Either way, he was my friend and he knew that I knew his game.

He is gone now to where there are no more tears, no more pain and no more run-ins with the law that was often unjust to my friend.

He will be missed by many. So on this day, I will say good-bye, not only for me, but for the many others who couldn't bear to say good-bye.

Mr. Cathey, rest in peace and the fun memories of you shall always be with me and all the others who loved you too. Good-bye, my friend, good-bye.

TIMOTHY'S DAY

Mr. Cathey's day has come and gone. We all went to celebrate his life and what a day it was. Folks were gathered to share his life story. Not a negative word was said about our dear friend Timothy.

There were folks standing, praising the Lord and saying amen like never heard of before. The preacher said, "Timothy was ready to leave this old world, where he will never have to say good-bye anymore, only howdy, howdy, howdy."

Life's celebration is a wonderful thing. It's a time to reflect upon a person's life and a time to inspire the living to embrace the Lord and renew their commitment to Jesus.

Life's celebration is like no other. We get the chance to share with the world things other folks may not have heard, things that we want others to know and personal secrets about the deceased on this day. The beauty of this celebration is that we learn what we already knew about Timothy, but from many others.

Life's celebration is something to embrace and not fear, for it is written that we must all face a day of life's celebrations. His memories and legacy shall live on in the hearts of many. Thank you, Timothy, for your love and friendship.

Embrace life, enjoy the world, renew your faith in God and prepare yourself for your own life's celebration! Oh, happy day.

HOW WILL I BE REMEMBERED

How will I be remembered? I don't know. I gave humanity all that I could give. I stood firm when others appeared weak. I fought battles that had no interest to me, but it did for others. I took on issues others would run from. I accepted criticism when it was unjust because folks couldn't understand what drove me to fight for justice.

How will I be remembered? I don't know. Life has many facets and aspects. Some things are placed before us and other things come upon us and we must decide what to do and what not to do. So how will I be remembered? I don't know.

Some will remember me for my kindness, my considerate attitude and my passion for others who needed my desire to help mankind. Others will remember me for my love for others, my love for them, my love for my family and my love for those I just met.

Others will remember my years as an advocate who was not afraid to fight *those who perceived they had power, those who intimidated others, or those whose position was of such that others dared not say anything,* yet with God on my side, I never wavered against justice or mankind.

Some will remember only my radical years, where I was given no other choice, but to stand for justice and equality regardless. But, I want the world to know I am human too. I made a few missteps along the way, probably jumped the gun on some issues, made many foes angry, or forced others to see the light. Either way, it didn't matter. I did what I thought was right.

How will I be remembered? I don't know. History will judge my actions, and God will judge my heart. That's how I hope I will be remembered.

Cedar Point
303 Yards →

The Centerpiece of Love is a collection of thoughts that intrigues the heart, mind and soul with love. The intent is to show how love can make the world go round and it will show how love can flow from the heart, mind and soul. It is just an example of what can happen when real love is in the mix, ending with the poem titled, "I Never Stopped Loving You."

"The Memorials" reminds us that love remains in our hearts, minds and souls after God calls our loved ones home. It represents the love, the respect, and the memories of moms, dads, brothers, sisters, nieces, nephews, cousins and friends. The last poem is titled, "How Will I Be Remembered." It reflects just how I want to be remembered when I am no longer on this side. It will make you think about your own life.

Pete Frierson is a paralegal for a nonprofit organization in Columbia, Tennessee. He is a civil rights leader and recently (2014) was awarded the Outstanding Civil Rights Advocate Award by the Columbia State Community College and Making a Difference Award by the South Central Abuse Coalition.

Pete is retired from the navy and enjoys traveling, camping, riding motorcycles and helping people.

He is also a member of Cambridge's Who's Who and past president of the Boys and Girls Club of America and he is a lifetime member of the Disabled Veterans, Fleet Reserve Association, Camping World and the National Association for the Advancement of Colored People.

He is a graduate of Columbia State Community College, where he graduated cum laude with an AA in marketing.